Cinderella
The Summer House

THIS HEAT IS **UNBEARABLE!** WE NEED TO FIND A WAY TO COOL DOWN.

A **SUMMER HOUSE** WOULD COOL YOU DOWN!

PERFECT! I'LL GIVE A PRIZE TO WHOMEVER BUILDS THE **BEST** ONE.

SOON, THE COURT BUILDERS WERE RUNNING AROUND HELPING EVERYONE WITH THEIR SUMMER HOUSE IDEAS.

2

3

WHILE CINDERELLA'S EYES WERE CLOSED, HER **FAIRY GODMOTHER** APPEARED AND WAVED HER WAND. IN A FLASH, A BEAUTIFUL BOAT RESTED ON THE WATER.

THERE YOU ARE! NOW ALL YOU NEED ARE SOME DECORATIONS.

OH, THIS IS WONDERFUL! THANK YOU.

WITH THE HELPS OF THE BIRDS, CINDERELLA CREATED A BEAUTIFUL WHITE CANOPY TO GIVE THE BOAT SOME SHADE.

JAQ AND GUS SCURRIED AROUND, ADDING SOFT CUSHIONS AND A WONDERFUL FEAST OF CHEESE AND FRUIT.

4

5

THE LITTLE MERMAID
The Doll's House

ONE DAY, ARIEL NOTICED THAT HER SISTERS SEEMED BORED . . .

THERE'S NOTHING *FUN* TO DO AT THE PALACE.

WHY DON'T WE GO OUT AND *FIND* SOME FUN, THEN?

SOON . . .

LOOK-- WE FOUND SOMETHING ALREADY!

ARIEL WAS THRILLED WHEN SHE SWAM INTO THE CABIN AND FOUND A FABULOUS *DOLL HOUSE* . . .

SCUTTLE CALLS THEM, ER, DOLLYWOGGLES, I THINK. OR DOLLS FOR SHORT. AND THEY HAVE LITTLE TINY DRESSES!

LOOK AT WHAT *ARIEL* FOUND! I WANT TO TRY.

ME, TOO!

CAREFUL, EVERYONE--THERE ARE ONLY *TWO* OF THEM AND *SEVEN* OF US!

YOU'VE BEEN PLAYING FOREVER. IT'S *MY* TURN!

HEY! NO FAIR, *AQUATA*--I JUST PUT THAT OUTFIT ON HER!

8

Butterfly Belle

IT WAS TIME FOR THE ANNUAL CARNIVAL IN BELLE'S VILLAGE! BELLE VISITED HER FATHER FOR THIS SPECIAL OCCASION...

LOOK, PAPA-- THERE'S A CONTEST FOR THE BEST FLOAT THIS YEAR!

WOULDN'T IT BE GREAT TO WIN AND LEAD THE PARADE?

IT WOULD! AND THERE'S ONLY ONE WAY TO DO IT. WHY DON'T *YOU* ENTER THE CONTEST, BELLE?

11

12

14

Jasmine
Perfect Parade

IT WAS NEARLY TIME FOR *THE SULTAN'S* CORONATION CELEBRATION AND *JASMINE* WANTED TO DO SOMETHING *EXTRA* SPECIAL THIS YEAR.

WE COULD ARRANGE A CORONATION PARADE THROUGH THE STREETS OF *AGRABAH*...

THAT'S A *SUPER* IDEA!

AUDITIONS FOR THE BIG PARADE WERE ORGANIZED RIGHT AWAY. EVERYONE IN AGRABAH WAS INVITED!

FROM THE START, THE AUDITIONS WERE VERY IMPRESSIVE . . .

ANYONE CAN CHARM A SNAKE-- BUT NOT TWO AT ONCE!

A JUGGLING LION? YOU'RE IN-- AND YOU CAN BRING YOUR HUMAN, TOO!

WE HAVE PLENTY OF DANCERS, BUT NONE OF THEM ARE ELEPHANTS!

OUR PARADE WILL BE UNFORGETTABLE!

you are cordially invited . . .

THE SULTAN SENT OUT INVITATIONS TO ALL HIS IMPORTANT FRIENDS.

ON THE DAY OF THE PARADE, THE SULTAN WAS VERY EXCITED.

MY GUESTS ARE GOING TO BE AMAZED!

COMIC STICKERS

ADD YOUR STICKERS TO YOUR POSTER OR ANYWHERE FUN!

JASMINE BEGAN TO DANCE AT THE FRONT OF THE PARADE. ALL OF THE PERFORMERS AND THEIR ANIMALS FOLLOWED HER.

JASMINE'S DANCING LOOKED LIKE SO MUCH FUN THAT, SOON, EVERYONE JOINED IN!

I KNEW OUR PARADE WOULD BE UNFORGETTABLE!

THE END!

21

THE RAINBOW PICKED UP AURORA, PHILLIP, AND THE FAIRIES, AND CARRIED THEM THROUGH THE FOREST.

SOON, THE FOREST LOOKED COLORFUL AND HAPPY AGAIN, AND THE FAIRIES FINALLY UNDERSTOOD THE BEAUTY OF NATURE. TO THANK AURORA FOR HER WISDOM, A FAIRY PLACED A FLOWER IN THE PRINCESS'S HAIR

...BUT IT SLIPPED AND FELL TO THE GROUND.

PRINCE PHILLIP TIED IT IN PLACE WITH THE RIBBON FROM THE PLATE. JUST THEN, THE RIBBON STARTED TO GLOW...

...AND THEY WERE BACK IN THE PALACE.

LOOKS LIKE WE'RE NOW A PART OF THE STORY, TOO!

AND IT LOOKS EVEN NICER THAT WAY!

THE END!

SOON...

MAYBE DADDY WOULD LIKE SOME ICE CREAM!

STEP RIGHT UP! EVERYONE ALWAYS FINDS OUR TREATS... *ENCHANTING.*

KING TRITON STARTED SNEEZING AND COULDN'T STOP...

WHEN *ANDRINA* AND *AQUATA* TRIED THEIR ICE CREAM, THEIR HAIR CHANGED COLOR...

ARISTA AND ALANA BROKE OUT IN RED SPOTS...

...WHILE *ADELLA* AND *ATTINA* COULDN'T STOP SWIMMING UPSIDE DOWN.

LUCKILY, ARIEL HADN'T TRIED HER ICE CREAM YET...

HOLD ON... THAT'S NO ICE CREAM MAKER. THAT'S *URSULA!*

Heh-heh-heh!

AND I BET *HER* CONE DOESN'T COME WITH A MAGIC SPELL.

Beauty and the Beast
A Perfect Match

ON THE ANNIVERSARY OF THEIR FIRST MEETING, *BELLE* AND *THE BEAST* BOTH WOKE UP WITH WONDERFUL PARTY IDEAS.

OVER BREAKFAST THEY EXPLAINED THEIR IDEAS TO EACH OTHER...

PINK AND FLUFFY IS JUST NOT MY STYLE, BELLE.

LET'S SEE IF WE CAN PLAN A PARTY USING BOTH IDEAS.

WILL YOU ALL HELP US?

29

SOON, IT WAS TIME FOR LUMIERE AND COGSWORTH TO HELP THE BEAST WITH *HIS* DECORATIONS.

IN THE MUSIC ROOM, CHIP HELPED BELLE REHEARSE HER PARTY SONG.

THEN IT WAS THE BEAST'S TURN...

≍OOF!≍ DO YOU WANT TO TELL HIM?

NO, I THINK *YOU* SHOULD!

MAYBE THIS *WASN'T* SUCH A GOOD IDEA, AFTER ALL.